THE
WORLD
COWERS

THE WORLD BURNS - BOOK 7

BOYD CRAVEN

The World Burns Book 7
By Boyd Craven

Many thanks to friends and family for keeping me writing!

TABLE OF CONTENTS

CHAPTER 1

W ho is this guy?" The President asked, reading a memo.

"A handyman and blogger. No military experience. It's his wife who's interesting," his aide slid a packet across the desk to the most powerful man in the world.

Months in the bunker had done little for their humor and color, yet the President seemed paler and grayer than he had just the past summer.

"Oh, wow. I didn't know we had female operatives of her caliber," he mused, closing the file after reading through the basics.

"Yes Sir, apparently the CIA has some as well, but she's bounced around between jobs. I think we're looking at the perfect storm here, boss. Right person, right time and bad luck. Sir, if the second

BOYD CRAVEN

hand rumors of your friend John Dav—"

"I thought we'd discussed that already, Patrick. John Davis and I went to school together a long time ago. He followed me to Chicago when I ran for the senate. Nobody shells a government official and gets away from it. According to him, he lost somewhere north of 75 to 80 men from engagements with this Homestead and the defections are much worse. No, we need to send a message and a strong response," the former Chicago senator said.

"Sir, if you'd at least consult with the joint chiefs on this, I think they'd—"

"Patrick, what is it you want me to do? You're going to argue against this no matter what, aren't you?"

"Sir, have you listened to the broadcasts? What if we let John Davis save face, and use this to our advantage? Play both sides of the fence and come out smelling like roses."

"What do you have in mind?" The President asked, leaning over the table.

"We make a point of stamping out this dissent so we don't have repeats, but we do it in such a way that we're doing it fairly. Right now, the way FEMA in the south and our own government and state officials have acted in certain situations has only made matters worse. We're at the brink of civil war. You take out a public figure like the Jacksons, it's going to cause a lot of grief for us. If we can figure something out—"

"Patrick, write it up. I've got a headache and I've

got a conference call with Davis. We're moving air assets to Kentucky to help him. You have two hours before I'm letting those Apaches fly."

"Sir, that's going to be a mistake."

"Noted. Again, you cannot shell a government official or murder his people who were acting under orders."

"Sir," Patrick said, sliding another folder, a much slimmer one than the Jackson's files to him, "This is what I'm talking about. I would use extreme caution if you move against the Homestead. It could have serious repercussions."

"Noted; I'll read this shortly. I've got a call to make. If that's all..." The President said, pushing his chair back and standing, offering his hand.

"No, it isn't, but it's imperative you read this before sending the Apaches to Kentucky," Patrick took the President's hand and then tapped the file folder the President was holding.

"I will. I've also got to talk with Justice Roberts, and he's in the Kentucky facility. He's a part of the panel there and he's insistent, so if you don't mind..."

"No, no. Thank you Sir," Patrick said, leaving.

If the former Supreme Court justice was involved, he felt there was a glimmer of hope. Maybe he could talk the President into looking into the allegations against his classmate, John Davis, aka Boss Hogg.

CHAPTER 2

"Blake, you have to hear this," David said, startling the man who'd been half dozing.

Blake had been on a week's worth of night watches, and was having a hard time staying up during the day time. Now that he was mostly healed, he didn't want everyone to think he wasn't pulling his fair share. There had been rumblings that the President was going to make the first announcement since the event happened. They'd been able to bring in a modest harvest, and it would take a lot of edge off the growing community and there was plenty to share with the survivors.

They had all speculated on who the President would be. It sounded like pretty common knowledge that the President and most of the House and Senate had fallen for one reason or another.

THE WORLD COWERS

"*Ladies and Gentlemen,*" the voice said and everyone sat up straight as the 44th President of the United States, the one believed to be dead spoke, "*I come here tonight, as your President and as a fellow human being, to talk to the citizens of our great nation.*

I'd like, first and foremost," he paused for a moment, "*to talk about the attack. There have been several points of misinformation that have been circulating. We were not attacked by Iran, Saudi Arabia, Iraq, Afghanistan or Syria despite what others have reported. They do not have the information that I do. It is true the nuclear talks were going badly, but it wasn't a single country that did this to us.*

Elements of ISIS and North Korea detonated a nuclear weapon over the United States of America in the guise of a satellite launch using a mobile sea platform. The resulting EMP has destroyed key critical infrastructure throughout most of the Continental United States, sparing some regions in the Pacific Northwest and Alaska. Our Canadian friends have suffered as well, in regions of Ontario and Quebec.

The regions of Mexico that have been touched by the EMP have already been experiencing destabilization from cartel violence, but they have not had the losses that we Americans have experienced. It's brutal, it's horrible and the reason you are not seeing the United States Military take more action within the country is because we are now fighting a war on two fronts.

First, the war against North Korea has begun

once again, as the Korean Armistice Agreement has been nullified. They've launched attacks against Washington DC, Maryland, and other parts of the Eastern seaboard. Even now, their subs try to sneak through our defensive networks. As we recall our military from around to globe to help in the naval battles, our country is being attacked from within.

There were elements in several cities, Dearborn and Ann Arbor Michigan for example, where there were radical religious factions that acted with the knowledge of the coming attack and destabilized the region. Those citizens and immigrants are being dealt with by a large force that has come down from Camp Grayling and from all over the Midwest. Acts of violence, terrorism and hate crimes are running rampant throughout the country. The racial violence in the States is staggering and, if there was ever a time for America to pull together, now is that time. Remember, neither race nor religion is a good enough reason to take up arms against your fellow humans.

There are, of course, more militant factions within the country; those who are born with radical conservative views who have openly refused orders and even attacked government agents and their leadership." Everyone stopped what they were doing, and Blake looked around the room, his eyes going wide.

"They can't be—" Sandra said, and she was shushed by Blake.

"*These factions will be stamped out and their leadership brought to justice. We will not tolerate former members of our armed services openly mocking* and attacking the government in their own homes and cities," he paused for a moment before continuing.

"As some of you may have already realized or heard, each Governor of the State has had the National Guard activated. All current and former service members between the ages of 18 and 65 are required to report for duty or evaluation, at the nearest National Guard outpost. I have heard reports of units going rogue and how things were settled, as the intelligence comes in to me slowly... but it will not be tolerated. Military members will report for duty or be prosecuted per executive order. Those men and women who betrayed their oaths... You will be dealt with as well.

Law Enforcement – I know many of you, like so many of the National Guard Units, have had to go home now to protect your families. It was your duty as a husband, wife, parent or guardian. Now it is time to guard our country, our cities, and our way of life. You are to report back to your stations and precincts where you will be resupplied by the FEMA emergency managers, who report to the Governors and myself. Martial Law is in effect until lifted by Executive Order, and all elections have been suspended.

"I..." the President paused again, "I really hope to suspend Martial Law as quickly as I can, because my advisors now tell me that over 80% of the country has died off in four separate waves. Those very sick or on life support, the ones taking life-saving medications, further more from disease and starvation and *lastly from human predation. I am asking everyone to assist with the rebuilding efforts, and for your co-operation with the Governors of the State.*

For those of you still in FEMA camps, I urge you to stay and continue the work. Some have told me that it's been called the equivalent of labor camps, or even concentration camps. I do not agree with that assessment. The horrors of a few isolated instances does not paint the picture of the entire effort of FEMA and NATO to help our nation getting kick started again. Without the labor to build critical components, we cannot pull ourselves out of the ashes. Instead of going to work, we're asking the people we're taking care of in the camps to do their part in contributing to rebuild our country.

Again, attacks against those camps will not be tolerated, and those who instigate or support them will be brought to justice." The words chilled everyone in the room. *"I want to stress to you, those in the camps are not prisoners, they are there to help with rebuilding key infrastructure, designed to help the population out."*

"...That is why with great regret, I have one last sad bit of news. The South West of the country is being invaded, for lack of a better term, by a private army whose members are from all over the world, seemingly financed by agents of ISIS and North Korea, being guided into the country by the Cartels. Texas, New Mexico, Arizona and parts of California are now open battlefields. There is very little information to go on now, and even if I had it I could not

share it openly before verifying its sources. We believe to be the start…" The President made another long pause, *"We believe it's the start of a land campaign that Americans haven't seen in many lifetimes. As soon as our Navy and Airforce bring personal and equipment back, they will be pressed into service defending our borders and key infrastructure.*

My fellow Americans, it is now time to take back our country and pull ourselves out of the ashes of a charred existence. I will be in touch. God Bless."

They all sat there in stunned silence for several heartbeats until Sandra's handset squawked. It had been set on the Rebel Radio Frequency, since everyone was monitoring the President's announcement. She fumbled to pick it up and keyed the mic.

"Sandra here, over?"

All eyes in the room turned to her.

"Sandra, this is John Davis here, the Governor you referred to as Boss Hogg. Do you copy me five by five?"

"Oh shit," Bobby whispered.

"Shut up," Duncan said, putting one beefy arm around Lisa, drawing her close.

"I read you, Governor," she said, her voice quaking.

"You have twenty minutes to turn yourself in with your husband or we'll wipe the Homestead off the map. I have three Apache Gunships en route now, as well as a Huey for your transport. You both will be arrested for treason, murder and war crimes. You will be tried by a combination of military and

11

civilian personnel. If found guilty, you will be executed. If you doubt my word, you should only have to look up. In a few moments."

Faintly from outside, people were letting out surprised yells. Everyone looked up as the sound of the choppers made it hard to hear.

"Furthermore, military units stationed at the Homestead, you have one week to pack and bring yourselves and your equipment to Greenville. Further acts of aggression will not be tolerated. If the orders are met, any past discretions will be forgiven and your lives will continue. If you do not follow these orders, it's unlikely that your lives will continue."

"That's putting us between a rock and a hard place," Sgt. Smith said angrily from the doorway.

"Shhhh," everyone chorused.

"Is that all?" Sandra asked.

"Publically. Now go to scramble," he said.

Sandra switched to the secure channel she said, "Continue."

"Now, I'd like you to know that your actions against me and my men have been noted by those above me. If you two weren't such public personas, I'd have used the gunships to scour your farms. I really hope you resist, because personally, I want to watch you both hang whether you're found guilty or not," Davis spat, his words full of venom.

"We have to give ourselves up," Blake said, pulling his wife close and wrapping his arms around her.

THE WORLD COWERS

"No," Lisa shouted, tears running down her eyes.

"Wait, if I don't tell the men and squad to stand down…" Sgt. Smith said, pulling the door open.

"Nobody fires on the choppers," Duncan shouted as Smith ran out the door.

"Chris?" Sandra called, and the little boy came running, almost leaping into his adopted mother's arms.

"Mommy, don't go," he said softly, the open door allowing the rotor wash to blow dusty wind into the house.

"I think I have to. Don't worry honey, I'll be home soon, besides, you're going to be helping out grandma," Sandra said, kissing him on the head and then putting him down.

"Daddy?" Chris asked.

"I have to go too. Don't you worry, I'll be back soon too. I think they're going to give me a ticket," Blake said, dropping a wink, "when I get back, we can play battleship some more."

He hoped it looked genuine, because he could now hear what everyone else outside had seen before they heard it. Chopper blades.

"He wasn't lying," Duncan yelled from the doorway.

Sandra keyed up her hand held on the tactical net, "Me and Blake are coming out unarmed. Nobody shoot, our end or your end Davis."

"Wise decision. Davis out."

Patty sobbed, then turned to the group, "I can't

let you go! First it was Neal and then your son," she said to Lisa, "and now they're taking you away for a kangaroo court trial! You can't!"

Patty launched herself towards the couple and almost bowled them over in a hug, her tears falling freely. They both hugged her back, hard.

"We have to, we can't do anything against three Apaches," Sandra told her, giving her the hand set.

They stripped themselves of their side arms and knives and walked towards the open door. The rotor wash from the helicopters was pushing the tall grass down in the field south of the house. A Huey like the one that had come a week earlier for Sandra was flaring for a landing.

"I love you," Sandra called over her shoulder, taking Blake's hand in his.

Blake turned, words escaping him. He knew this day may come, but the double or triple shock of the message took the words right out of his mouth. They knew their actions would have repercussions if the government ever re-organized but they had felt they had acted just. Now they were sending three Apache's as a show of force? Blake felt like it was threatening an anthill with a bazooka. There was no way the Homestead could easily defeat three flying war machines.

"There they are," Sandra said, pointing with her free hand.

The choppers were at three points of the compass, their armaments all pointing towards the heart of the Homestead. Thankfully, there weren't very many people outside. Blake figured they would have all hidden in the barracks; but that could turn into their grave if the Apache's opened up, dropping the barn on top of them.

"I see them," He said, his voice coming out dry, his voice cracking.

"Are you scared?" She asked him.

"Terrified. You?"

"Nope," She pulled him close and kissed him on the cheek.

"Liar," Blake teased as four armed men dropped out of the helicopter, their guns raised.

Blake and Sandra kneeled, with their hands over their head and were quickly frisked, then cuffed. After all they had done, they were surprised at how they were handled. It wasn't the rough and painful treatment Blake had been expecting, but it seemed like more of a formality than an arrest by the way the soldiers acted.

From around the Homestead, people watched, many of them with guns at the ready, even if it would be suicidal to open or return fire.

§ § §

"It's my fault," Duncan said, grabbing the handset from Patty.

"Silverman, this is Duncan, over?" Duncan said into the radio on the frequency they'd set aside for both units to talk with.

"Silverman, this is Duncan, are you there?

15

Over?"

Again, silence.

"The militia…?" Lisa asked.

"I hope to hell… Ouch," Duncan said, grabbing his arm after Lisa delivered a healthy pinch, "I hope to heck that Davis hasn't moved against them." Duncan said.

"What if they just turned themselves in, you know, once they heard the President?" David asked, trying to comfort a still crying Patty.

"I don't know, we need to send a team over there and check. I'll let Smith handle that when he gets his troops calmed down and explains what he has to. My God man, we have a mess," Duncan said, his voice rising.

The portly preacher's color was rising, and he rubbed his shoulder.

"Sit down," Lisa said, noticing his discomfort, "you're going to work yourself into a heart attack," she cautioned.

Duncan had been struggling with his blood pressure, and even medicated it had been dangerously high. He'd lost a lot of the weight during the 'survival' diet and getting a lot of exercise, but the damage to his body had accumulated over the years.

"I…" Duncan went to the couch and sat down, closing his eyes, "We were all comfortable, ready. The threat had been eliminated. This is just too damned sudden, it happened too quick. That level of organization would take a lot of coordination and we heard nothing about it."

THE WORLD COWERS

"It was unexpected, and we have to get our kids back," Lisa said, sitting down by his side.

"My daughter's pregnant. I can't…"

"Calm down, it's going to be fine. We'll get them back."

They had all been shocked at the sudden arrival of the Apaches, hadn't even realized there were any in the area, but then again that's what they were known for. Fast, quiet and deadly. There had been three of them, more than enough to have leveled the Homestead.

§ § §

"This way Sir, Ma'am." The soldier holding them at gunpoint directed them to the open door.

They'd landed in what appeared to be an old quarry. Kentucky was lousy with hills, rocks and coal. What had been even more surprising upon landing had been seeing a steel blast door set into the side of the wall, already sliding open from a hidden mechanism.

"What the…" Blake said.

"DUMB," Sandra told him.

"I know it's dumb, I mean, look at it, but did you know it was here?"

"Deep Underground Military Base?" Sandra asked the soldier.

"Yes Ma'am, this one is part of the COOP," he told her, using the tip of his gun to point towards the open doorway.

"Oh boy," Blake said, "you two so need to fill me in on this."

"Continuity of Operations," Sandra told him, "Part of FEMA."

"I figured it meant something like that. This isn't Greenville, that's for sure."

"Yeah, we sure aren't in Kansas anymore Toto," Sandra told him, coming to a stop just inside the door where three soldiers had been standing, their guns pointing at them.

"It'll be explained to you shortly, then your de-briefing and then your trial," the soldier behind them said, the last words spat out as if he'd tasted something bad.

"Not a fan of the Governor?" Blake asked, guessing.

"I am one of Silverman's former teammates," he told them, making them both jerk their heads around and making the three soldiers standing in front of them very nervous.

"We just saw him a week or two ago, you were with him or—"

"I was. Listen, I don't have time to talk, but things are really weird and I can't explain. It's way above my pay grade. PFC Sherman here," he told them nodding.

"Tank, I bet they called you Tank," Sandra told him before turning and facing forward.

"Good guess," Tank whispered from behind them, and then much louder, "Prisoners Blake and Sandra Jackson, as ordered.

18

THE WORLD COWERS

"Take them to holding."

"What is this place exactly?" Blake asked Sandra, trying not to take his eyes off the guns in front of him.

"A big bunker, basically." Sandra told him quietly as they were led deeper into the rock.

The walls looked like painted steel plates, riveted at the seams, with exposed columns and beams in the larger sections of the hall. They passed through two checkpoints inside, all manned by different sets of guards. Eventually, without passing anyone else, they came to a room with keycard access. With a start, Blake realized the thing that had been bugging him but he couldn't figure out… it was the unnatural light. It'd been months since the EMP and he hadn't seen lights. These guys had power, and things worked.

The door opened, and they were ushered inside. Four holding cells lined one wall immediately across from them, with two rooms at either end. One of them was marked as a unisex bathroom. Steel folding chairs lined one side, where a small white end table with a stack of magazines sat. A water cooler sat, humming silently while it was obviously running. Blake and Sandra had running water from Blake's well and hot water from his low tech water heater, but cooled chilled water?

Blake realized how much he'd taken his power for granted. He'd known up front he was going to have to make sacrifices in order to install his solar setup, but this room made things look as if nothing

BOYD CRAVEN

had happened. It was staggering.

"In there, Ma'am," Tank pointed to the open door to the middle cell.

Blake noticed a sleeping form on the far end, in the last cell, next to the unmarked door.

"You're in here Sir," Blake was motioned into a cell next to Sandra's, and he stepped in.

"But why can't I—"

"Sorry Sir, orders. Someone will be with you shortly," PFC Sherman turned and left the room, followed by the three guards who'd helped escort them the entire way.

"Well isn't this some shit," the sleeping form said, a thin blanket falling away.

Silverman sat up, rubbing sleep from his eyes and looked at the pair of them.

"Sgt. Silverman?" Sandra asked.

CHAPTER 3

"I can hardly wait for this trial to start," Davis said, running his thick meaty hands together as his assistant Pamela fretted over his notes.

"Mr. Davis, it's a mockery of a trial. They plainly sent men to kill you. Even played rock music over the radio waves as they shelled the town," Pamela said.

"The school command post," Davis corrected her.

"Luckily we were already out of the area. I'm glad some of your men stayed loyal," she said.

In truth, she was glad because she'd been assigned to him and it had been one of the only things keeping her safe, as long as she could keep him away from her bed. He'd hinted and outright asked once, but she was hearing rumors. There wasn't any way she'd been hungry or desperate enough to cave in like so many of the others had.

"Yes, as soon as we're through with these hicks, I'll use the time I have the Apaches on loan to quell the riots in Louisville. A show of force, like we did at the Homestead, will go a long way to making sure things look legitimate and on the up and up."

"Do you expect the trial to go rather quickly?" Pamela asked.

"Sure, it was broadcast live, over our own airwaves and the publics. They blasted the damned music while keeping their tactical nets going. There's no denying it. I just wish we'd been able to capture Sandra like we'd tried. We lost some damned good men that day, before they used our own government's artillery on us."

"Why was it important to capture her? You never were clear on that, Sir."

"Because," Davis said, using a monogrammed handkerchief to wipe his sweaty bow, "She's the brains of the group. What they did to us was all brute force, no cunning. It was the worst embarrassment I've ever had, even trumping the first encounter with them," Davis told her, his voice rising in anger at the end, "If it had been her running that operation, she would have had me killed. I'm sure of it."

"Well, very soon you can confront them in front of the panel, and let your position be known. But Sir... There is another matter, something for the trial..." Pamela said, her words trailing off.

THE WORLD COWERS

"Yes?" Davis asked, confused at her tone and change in demeanor.

"Your character is going to be called into question. The way you were micromanaging Sgt. Silverman's units before their defections and the rumors of what goes on…" Pamela hesitated and swallowed down a big lump that was forming in her throat.

"A rumor of what?" Davis asked her, noticing her shift in attitude.

Fear? Was she afraid to speak her mind?

"It's just that… There are rumors of your improprieties circulating. Sir." Pamela said, scared she'd gone too far.

"*He had to have heard of them,*" she thought to herself.

"Improprieties? You mean the angry husband who's been shouting threats because his wife visited me? I didn't know she was married."

"It's the circumstances of hers were unfortunate. Apparently the husband is claiming she traded you… uh… well, for antibiotics for her children that were sick."

"There was no trading involved there," Davis said, "She came on to me and that's that. When she told me her kids were sick, I made sure she had access to the medical technicians that were part of the guard unit. Nobody wants to see sick kids dying for lack of a dollars' worth of penicillin."

"Sir, if this were the only case—"

"Pamela, why are you trying my patience? Aren't I good to you?" Davis asked, a hint of annoyance in his voice.

"Sir, I—"

"You know, you being my personal assistant means that you've lived in a comfortable lifestyle while others in our country have not. It's very possible that without me, you'd be out there, alone. A part of the unwashed masses, scrambling for food, doing what you need to do to survive," Davis said, taking a drink of a diet coke.

The condensation coming off the can distracted Pam's eyes. She hadn't been afforded the luxury of a pop in a long while, yet Davis seemed to have a stash that he'd guarded jealously.

"I suppose you're right," she said softly, not sure if that was a veiled threat.

"Oh I know it. You never know, without me," he rose and walked behind her, dropping his hands on her shoulders, moving her long black hair off her left shoulder, "you would probably be out there alone, doing a lot of whatever you had to do to survive. Maybe you should be nicer and more appreciative. You're on my side here," Davis said, his hand rubbing circles over her shoulder and slowly down the front—

"Sir," she said, sliding her chair back, hitting the Governor in the ample stomach he sported.

She leapt to her feet, taking a few steps back, getting space between Davis and herself. He hadn't gone too far, but only by a small hair's breadth.

"I'm sorry Pamela. I didn't mean that to... well... you and I have been so close for months.

THE WORLD COWERS

I can't help if I'm somewhat attracted to you. You don't have a husband or boyfriend. I do apologize, I thought that it was because you'd—"

"Sir, I'm sorry, but I don't like you like that."

"Then it was a mistake on my part," Davis said, sitting back down and downing the remaining Coke in one long swallow.

"A mistake, Sir?" she asked, her voice going soft now that he'd given her a plausible excuse.

She halfway believed him, too. She wasn't attracted to the man, not one bit. She'd appreciated the relative safety that being his assistant allowed, but warming his bed was not in her job description – and it would never be.

"Yes, a mistake. I thought you were ready. After this trial is done and we get the State back in order, I'm going to need a strong woman at my side. I was rather hoping that woman would be you."

"*A strong woman at his side?*" she thought to herself, "*wasn't she already on his side? Just not the bedside.*"

"Perhaps, Sir. I must get ready, your general counsel will be sitting in on this meeting or trial. He'll be there already, if I know him."

"Don't you worry," Davis told her, "I've got the President's backing. We were old schoolmates and I, of course, run the state by his graces and wishes."

"I'm not worried, Sir. I don't think you're taking this seriously enough." Pamela told him, stepping around him and getting to the doorway.

"Oh, I'll take it seriously. In that thought, give

my offer some thought. I'd like for you to seriously consider my offer. A woman like you at my side would have all the comforts of a normal life, or one much, much better." Davis said, giving her his best politician's smile.

"I'll consider it, Sir," she said and left the room.

"Idiot," she told the empty corridor, her body breaking out in delayed gooseflesh after his hands had touched the skin of her neck.

The contact had revolted her and, though he hadn't come out and said anything that could be misconstrued as improper, the threat was implied, and she could feel the pressure of his offer.

"No way," she murmured to herself, "not this girl."

CHAPTER 4

"What... how?" Blake asked him, sitting on the cot that ran through the back of each of the cells.

There was one empty cell between them, but they were less than ten feet apart.

"They came in yesterday. We'd been ordered to stand down. The orders didn't come from Davis, but higher up the chain of command."

"They just came out of the woodwork? Just like that?" Sandra asked, shocked that it had happened and they hadn't overheard it over the radio chatter.

"Helicopters. They have been pretty accommodating actually. The guards will be in every few hours to let me use the restroom or bring food. It's just damned boring in here."

"How didn't we hear any of it? Why didn't you

alert us?" Blake asked.

"Happened so quickly, we were ordered to radio silence. When my old CO stepped off the Huey, I knew I was in trouble."

"Did you hear the President's announcement?" Sandra asked.

"Yeah, they piped it in here a couple hours ago. I guess we're the dissidents that attacked a government leader?"

"Yeah," Blake said, "but you weren't a part of that."

"Oh bull, I led two teams and families away from the chaos. We talked about this, man. It's treason or dereliction of duty for doing what I did, knowing what was going to happen."

"You were following your oath, not some delusions from a sweaty old man," Sandra reminded him, "He wasn't even military. He micromanaged everything you guys were doing—"

"Getting men killed. Thankfully it was the mercs he sent. Otherwise it would have been worse on you guys," Silverman said, standing and stretching.

"Depends on who you ask," Blake said quietly, "it was a slaughter. Nobody can keep doing that and not be affected. Nobody good that is."

"I know, but sooner or later, he's going to run out of cannon fodder, or the rest of the men are going to do what we did. Get out of the way. Nobody wants to die for no good reason."

"Is there ever a good reason to die?" Blake asked him, and was shocked when it was Sandra who responded.

"You don't die for a reason, you die for your brothers and sisters in arms. When you're 'in the shit', you don't worry about your oath, your rules and regs, not even the rules of engagement. You're fighting so your buddy next to you doesn't bite it. He's fighting so you don't get killed. It's complicated and weird. Hive mind type of stuff." Sandra said.

"Wow," Blake said softly.

"Oh look, it's time for the party to start," Silverman said, smiling.

The door they'd been led through opened and a slightly built man walked in. He wasn't in uniform, but a charcoal gray suit. His dark hair was parted on the left side and his glasses looked like the blocky black framed ones that were popular in an older era. When PFC Sherman accompanied him into the room, Blake lost it and started to laugh.

"What are you doing?" Sandra asked out of the side of her mouth, moving closer to her right, to be nearer Blake.

"Who does that guy look like?" Blake asked, between the unmanly giggles.

"Somebody important," she growled.

The man stopped in front of Blake, smiling deeply.

"I am rather curious," the man said, a heavily accented Texas drawl, "what it is that amuses you so?"

"Don't," Sandra said, loudly this time.

"It's just that—"

"Blake," she almost shouted.

The man turned and held up a hand, as if to beg her a moment.

"I am curious, merely to see if his sense of humor matches mine," he turned to Blake.

"It's just that with Sherman there, and you... you must be Mr. Peabody?" Blake asked and Silverman let out a surprised guffaw before stopping himself.

Blake stole a glance over to Sandra whose eyes had gone wide and then they all lost it and laughed. Surprising everyone, Mr. Peabody joined in as well, until he took the black-framed glasses off and cleaned them on his white shirt.

"That's what I thought. My glasses got broke early on in the event, and I was issued these. I think they're to be used on people that want to become poster children for abstinence." They all lost it then, with his admission.

Silverman sat down on his cot, wiping his eyes and Blake smiled, starting to get himself under control. In the world where there wasn't much to laugh about, the rare instances where you did, you let it out.

"Now listen here," he said, the word here almost coming out "hea", "I'm told you three are to go in front of a military tribunal. It's not actually that, it's a panel of five. I'm supposed to be representing you all, " he said, but you could hear the y'all in his voice, "and things aren't as usual or ordinary as I'd like them to be. First things first. My name's Martin

THE WORLD COWERS

Cates, like the woman's name Kate with an S on the end of it."

"Mister Cates," Blake said, sticking his hand out between the bars to shake.

He noticed that of everyone in the room, PFC Sherman was the only one who'd kept his composure.

"Mr. Jackson. Missus Jackson," he said moving over one to take her hand in both of his, not in a handshake, but one hand over the other before dropping the grip and moving down to Silverman.

"Sgt. Silverman," he said, giving the man a shake.

"Sir," Silverman replied.

"So…" Blake asked after a while, "You're our… public defender?"

"Something like that, but more like an advocate," he said, dragging a metal chair to within a few feet of the bars, sitting down and pulling out a clipboard with a pad of paper.

"Now, I need you all to fill me in. Start at the beginning," he said, his pen clicking as he bowed his head down to start writing.

"The beginning where we met Boss Hogg?" Blake asked.

"Oh, man… You're talking about Davis aren't you?" Cates said, looking up and smiling.

"Yeah," Sandra told him, remembering the day they had met him.

"No, before that. I know Mr. Silverman's life when the EMP happened, it's all on record. I want to hear yours, and then we'll go through what happened with Davis and the mercenaries he sent after your teams and families.

Silverman sat up in surprise, "They never sent anyone after us," he said.

"Twenty men. They never came back," Cates told him, "That's one of the charges against you and your men. Twenty men lost or killed by you and yours."

"That's absurd, they sent them against... Oh hell, this isn't going to be a normal military trial, is it?"

"No Sir, I don't believe it is. The circumstances are rather curious, and nothing like this has been done legally before," Cates told them, putting pen to paper, "Now Blake, would you like to go first?"

§ § §

Duncan had calmed greatly, but Martha and Lisa were ready to sit on him if needed to hold him down. It finally took Bobby and Sgt. Smith to talk to him, to make him rest. It had been close; the pain in his chest had flared up so suddenly and so hard, it'd started to take his breath away. He'd felt nauseated but, once he sat down, he didn't quite feel so bad. Chris had immediately taken it as a sign that grandpa wanted to rough house and that was quickly stopped, though it'd made Duncan laugh.

"Teams are reporting in," David told them, "their radio equipment was taken and the top men were escorted out by helicopters yesterday. They're breaking camp and the men are fixing to return to… Greenville? The families that are staying behind have asked if they can join The Homestead."

"We can wait for him to get back to get the report," Duncan said. "Besides, we have to have a meeting."

"Who all are we asking?" Lisa said, running her fingers through her husband's hair lightly.

"All active and former military and law enforcement. We've taken in and absorbed a lot of folks before and after John Davis. We need to find out how many—"

"Duncan, Mom, "Bobby interrupted, "I'm still doing the census polls as people come in. You know we converted a lot of the barn loft into sleeping space, well, that along with the barracks and trailers has us at close to one hundred thirty men, women and children." Bobby said.

It'd been his job originally, when he'd gotten bashed in the head, and had been set up accidentally by his fiancée before they'd become an item. The concussion had left him hurting for days, but meeting and talking to the new people they'd rescued had been what he could do to help. He still did it, and kept his records in a dog eared notebook he'd found in a pile of boxes. He'd been the one who had worked out the shared bed routine, like the old Navy term, 'hot cot'.

"How many former or active troops are living with Sgt. Smith's men now?" Duncan asked.

Ever since Smith had split off from the rogue unit, they'd set up their own small camp in the wooded area to the west of the big field. They'd done so when it became apparent that they needed a place to stay. They had brought their own equipment, armaments and sleeping arrangements. The numbers in there swelled as single men who had once been in service, found living with them seemed more comfortable and familiar than a basement of a barn.

"Forty three," Bobby told him, "Then if you count us, the core group," Bobby said, motioning to the room….

"Wow, I never realized that there were so many of us now," Patty said.

"There's more kids and young people up to nineteen years of age than us adults," Bobby told them, "lots of them lost parents or caregivers."

"So we gots new mommies and daddies," Chris said, and his face fell as the realization hit him. "Do I have to get a new Mommy and Daddy now that—"

"Shhhh," Lisa said, pulling him into her lap, "We told you, it won't be long."

"Ok," Duncan said, sitting up from where he'd been laying on the couch, "Bobby, go ahead and call a general meeting. Whoever's manning the OPs can stay and I'll talk to them personally, but we need to figure this out. If Davis is still in charge and the orders are legit, we need to make a decision - and fast."

THE WORLD COWERS

§ § §

"What I've been told," Cates said, "is that this is going to be more like a moderated discussion rather than a civilian or military trial."

"Why is that?" Silverman asked.

"Why are they even giving us a trial?" Sandra cut in.

"Here's how I see it," Cates said, standing and stretching, "you all are somewhat public figures and have put the call out, so to speak, to have people start moving towards the heartland of America. Would you be surprised to hear that many are doing so?"

"Yes," Blake said simply.

"Would it surprise you to hear that the informal network of agents working in the south, in Alabama, Louisiana and other Gulf states, wouldn't have gotten together if it hadn't been for Rebel Radio and a guy named John?"

"Yes," Sandra said this time.

"Would it surprise you to hear that most of the police and military personnel in this country agree with what you and yours have done? I mean, in every case it seems like you've all gotten the worst of the worst and dealt with it."

"We're just acting as our consciences allow." Blake told him.

"I was acting under the oath I took," Silverman told him, "Even though martial law supposedly trumps all of our rights."

"I was acting with both," Sandra told them, "as former military and as a human, I did what I felt was right. Every time."

"So I'm going to mark that one down as a yes," Cates said, "These are all good things in your favor. The panel you're going to be sitting in front of will include the head of FEMA for the state of Kentucky, two military men and one woman of high rank. I don't know most of them so don't ask... oh, and a former Kentucky Supreme court judge. He's the one I think you're gonna like, Ma'am."

"Why's that?" Sandra asked.

"He's the one who insisted you both be handled with the utmost care, and that your delicate condition not be compromised." Cates told them, taking his glasses off and rubbing the red mark across his nose.

"He means the baby," Blake said.

"I know that, dummy," Sandra snarked.

"Is that what happened with me?" Silverman asked, "They didn't fire or even attack, just swooped in and demanded our surrender. They took me and a few of my men, but left the rest, including their equipment, with orders to report for duty."

"I think that may have also come from him as well. He's not a fan of John Davis," Cates said, putting the glasses back on.

"Where is the Governor in all of this?" Blake asked, "He sounded like we were to be fitted with a noose right away."

"He's... difficult. He's going to be the star of the

THE WORLD COWERS

prosecution. Hell, he is the prosecution. He's furious that the President has asked for this panel to do the trial. It was either that or admit he'd been wrong to appoint Davis, and put someone else in charge. There have also been some nasty rumors about him so… Since Davis was… or is… a personal friend of the President's—"

"Crony politics at its best," Blake finished.

"Yes Sir," Cates said. "It's as much for his benefit as it is yours."

"When do we… I mean, what… The trial?"

"You're in the dark as much as I am. I'm just a criminal defense attorney, one who volunteered to sit in this case."

"How does a Texan, a civilian at that, get invited into a DUMB?" Silverman asked, curious.

"My wife's rank," he said, smiling. "My wife's one of the military personnel sitting on the panel of judges."

"So you're not as much in the dark as you let on?" Blake asked.

Relief flooded through Blake, and he almost shook in relief. Cates's easy demeanor and soothing voice had done a lot to put them at ease, but what he said next almost shattered that.

"She is a stickler for rules and orders. Don't think that she's going to go easy on y'all because I happen to think they should set ya free. I've argued your case to her dozens of times and not won one yet."

"We're on our own here, aren't we?" Sandra

asked, rubbing her stomach.

"We always have been, darling," Cates told them, putting the chair up against the wall where the others were.

"Well that sucks." Blake said, sitting back on the cot and then laying down.

"When does the trial start?" Silverman asked.

"Soon," Cates told them.

"Lovely," Sandra said, sitting on her own cot.

"Food will be brought to you all soon, and somebody will be here for restroom breaks. I'll have some clean clothing brought to you here - and don't worry, it isn't prison orange," Cates told them, leaving the room, followed by Sherman.

"That was weird," Sgt. Silverman said.

"Tell me about it," Blake told him.

CHAPTER 5

... **W**e've all heard rumblings about the attacks in the Southwest, especially in light of the folks released from the FEMA camps, many of which couldn't or wouldn't return home to the even more dangerous areas," Sgt. Smith said to the assembled crowd.

They were gathered loosely in a semicircle around him on the hill. He stood downslope so everyone could see and hear him. Small children were hushed, but even with the news, there was still some playfulness in the air as parents smiled at their antics.

"It appears that we've been repeating a lot of bad information, me included. When the grid went down, so did the communications for a lot of us.

Now, I used to be active duty, but had gotten back into the National Guard to finish things out. I was on patrol and had been tasked with helping track down some folks when I had a… disagreement with my commanding officer. I'll probably face a court martial no matter what, for what I did and my actions, whether they were justified or not.

The reason I'm sharing this, is that many of you – and myself – are now being recalled to active duty. They've given us one week to report in. I do not say this lightly, but I heard the President's speech with my own ears. I've even met the man once, when he was running. Our old comm channels are now back and working and there are no longer strangers with the wrong passcodes and information on them. I'll never know if they were NATO, imposters or some-body who stumbled across some hardware, but my last communication checks out and it was a legiti-mate order to return to base."

He let that sink in.

"What about our families?" a man asked from the crowd, not one of Smith's men.

"I will have to defer that to Duncan and Lisa, since they took Blake and Sandra for interrogation, though they've consented to let the families of Sgt. Silverman's men come to live here." Smith said and instantly wished he could have taken it back.

It was a hornet's nest issue, and many voices were raised and vile threats made.

"Why aren't we planning a rescue?" a woman screamed, the mother of one of the younger women

THE WORLD COWERS

they had saved from the slavers.

"We don't know where they are exactly, and honestly, this is a legal and legitimate order. Whether or not we follow our oaths is a personal decision, but it's one that can affect the group."

"If all the former and current soldiers leave, who'll protect us?" a woman shouted.

"I don't have answers at this time, I just wanted to inform you of the broadcast and leave you with the information I got so you can all make your decisions. I suggest we meet tomorrow night and discuss this further," Smith told them, trying to wrap things up before it got ugly.

Blake and Sandra had personally helped or save many within the group, and had almost become cult leaders of a small tribe. They didn't want it, but it was eerie and scary to Smith and Duncan who'd discussed just this at length.

"So why not—"

"I'm sorry, I do not have answers. I'm wrestling with these things myself. I just happen to have the loudest mouth in the group tonight," Smith said and walked uphill through the crowd. Many tried to pause him, to engage him with more questions, but he kept going.

He didn't even know what he wanted to do himself. He was torn and, if he didn't know what he wanted to do, he couldn't even begin answering for others. He was out of his element and wished he had Sandra to help guide and direct. Duncan was good, but he'd had a close call and Smith didn't want to pressure the big man more than he already was. He was going to sleep on it, and then ask his friends in his unit.

§ § §

"I still feel like we're walking to our execution," Silverman griped.

They were being led down a nondescript hallway by Sherman, with Cates walking within the group. They'd gone over their basic timelines again and he'd told them to just tell the truth. It seemed so simple, but no matter what they said, Davis's words loomed over them and they were scared. It wasn't even the fact that it wasn't a real trial, it was the uncertainty of it. Would Cates's wife hold her husband's defense of them against the trio?

"It's unreal," Blake said.

"What?" Sandra asked, putting an arm around him and hugging him with one arm.

"We were sitting safe, thinking that everything was ok in the world, or at least our little part. No more bad guys, no more rogue agents... We even got the harvest in. If Hogg hadn't kept attacking us, we would have had tons of food to share. Metric tons. Heck we still do... and to have three helicopters come and swoop us up with no warning?"

"I never planned for that," Sandra said softly, "one maybe... if we played dirty, but not three. If they were going to send that much force... I just hope Davis didn't flip flop on his word and level the

Homestead," Sandra said, her words hitching in her throat.

"He didn't. He's got somebody watching his actions for the time being," Cates told her. "We're almost there. Is there anything I can say to put your minds at ease? My wife assures me that they're all going to judge this fairly, and it'll take a majority vote to convict or acquit."

"That in itself is actually comforting Sir," Silverman said quietly.

"Then let's get this dog and pony show over," Blake said as they paused at a door.

Sherman's keycard let them in and they were surprised to be led into a utilitarian-looking conference room with a large oval shaped table. At one end sat the four men and one woman, three of them in uniform. On the other side of the table on the right was John Davis, accompanied by a man and woman. The three of them were dressed in expensive looking suits.

The woman sitting next to Davis looked to the group as they came in and gave them a weak half smile before turning to gaze at the judges.

"Here we are," Cates said, putting his notepad on the seat towards the middle so Silverman, Blake and Sandra would be to his left, buffering them from Davis.

Davis gave each of them a death glare, conveying all his thoughts with one foul look.

"Please, be seated. Tank, make sure we're not interrupted," the woman wearing a military uniform instructed their guard.

"Yes Ma'am," PFC Sherman closed the door behind them after giving Silverman a smile and a whispered 'good luck Sarge.'

The electronic lock clicked closed and everyone turned and stared at each other.

"This is going to be the most difficult case I've ever heard. I'm Justice Stevens, formerly of the Kentucky Supreme Court, retired. To my right is Major Roberts, then Lt. Commander Sola, Commander Cates and Director of FEMA for the state of Kentucky Mr. Franklin Hines."

"Sirs and Ma'am," Cates said, tipping an imaginary hat at them.

Commander Cates frowned at him and then turned to look at the Governor, "This trial or hearing has been set up for two reasons: first, to clear the air. I understand you went to school with the President and consider him a friend," Cates said to Davis. "That has no bearing in this hearing, nor will the good old boys system sway me or anyone else here. You're charging that the Jacksons and Sgt. Silverman committed an act of treason, causing you and your men loss of equipment, life and property.

"Mr. and Mrs. Jackson," she continued, "we've monitored your broadcasts from almost the beginning, being sequestered in this base. You've become somewhat local celebrities, even more so than you realize. Your call to action in discussing the Governors actions was highly inflammatory and we're starting to see civil unrest across the nation. If we do nothing about you, we're seen as going along with what you've done. If we are to execute you, you die a martyr and the civil unrest becomes overwhelming across the nation."

Those words sent a shiver down Blake's spine and he tried not to look at his wife, afraid of showing her how much fear he felt.

"Furthermore, your call to action also alerted us to the fact that government offices may have been abused, something we'd not read about in our weekly reports from Mr. Davis. When we got word that Sgt. Silverman had split off and left with his unit's families, we became interested in the truth of the situation. Gentlemen and women, it's time to get to the bottom of this and move forward, hopefully in a direction the country can manage to live with."

"Mr. Davis would like to speak," the man sitting next to the Governor said, and the panel nodded and waited.

John Davis, aka Boss Hogg, stood. He was wearing a dark gray suit that was bursting at the seams, and even in the cool damp subterranean air, he was sweating, possibly from nerves.

"Sirs and Ma'am," he said, "I was given the job of Governor of the State to bring about order, to make sure the people were kept fed and clothed, and to re-establish government order. We also became aware of Blake Jackson and his wife's group of survivors through the radio transmissions. Through listening in and the conversations, we noted their location and planned on talking with them as my Guard went through the areas, rescuing people, obtaining supplies and feeding the hungry and starving folks in our state.

It was the same job we'd been doing since the crisis happened, but because of the popularity of Mr. Jackson and his lovely wife, I rode myself to meet them. They met us at gunpoint, ambushing me and my men. They disarmed us, blew up my command Humvee and spread dissent within my men, demoralizing them. I had only insisted in helping with relocating survivors and inventorying food for redistribution. Again, the same job I'd been doing since the event happened. I promised them I would be back to enforce the executive order I was given, as pursuant to my job and appointed by the President of the United States of America.

Sending my men in, they were ambushed, slaughtered and equipment stolen. Later, they would encourage Sgt. Silverman here to defect with his men and equipment and then they blew up my command post at the old school. I fled here to go into hiding until I could regroup - and here we are."

"Thank you Mr. Davis, please sit," Justice Stevens said.

Davis hesitated a moment, and then took his chair.

"Since I seem to be representing three of the accused, who would you like to talk to first?" Mr. Cates asked the panel.

"Although I am curious to hear from Sgt. Sil-

THE WORLD COWERS

verman directly," Major Roberts said, "I think for chronological reasons, I'd like to hear from Mr. and Mrs. Jackson first," he said looking around.

Blake stood and cleared his throat, and was joined by Sandra a moment later who took his left hand, intertwining her fingers with his. The formerly solitary man felt the weight of their stares and looked around the room. He tried to begin, but just a squeak came out. Lt. Commander Sola motioned him to lean in and he handed Blake a glass of ice water. He took a sip and cleared his throat.

"Sorry, I'm a little nervous here, Sirs and Ma'am."

"That's fine, go on," Director Himes said.

"Since the event happened, all we've been doing is trying to survive. We've been attacked by criminals who'd been released from jail, on two occasions I think, we've rescued a harems worth of women from a group who was using them for sexual slavery... and they were connected to a rogue National Guard unit. Sgt. Smith split from that unit when it was deployed to our area and, being new to Gerard's command, they became a part of our unit and helped us defeat Gerard and a group of cannibals. We've lost men and women along the way. I myself have been shot twice, healed, and helped find survivors...

Despite what Mr. Davis thought, we were not hoarding stores and stores of food that could feed the city. I simply had enough there to help the people I had with me."

"How many people is that?" Sola asked.

"Almost two hundred," Sandra said, giving his hand a squeeze.

There were quiet mutterings amongst the panel who leaned back and discussed things. Even though they were literally just across the table, Blake and Sandra couldn't make out their words.

"That takes a tremendous amount of food to feed that many. How were you able to provide so much?" Commander Cates asked.

Blake took that question to be his so he spoke up first, "Ma'am, when it was just a few of us, and then the Cayhills... we expanded the garden and hunted and trapped a bit. I have a root cellar that I'd keep the root veggies good in for a long while. We kept expanding the gardens. As more people joined the group, we sent out search parties for both food and survivors. Right away, we hit pay dirt on the interstate. We found a food truck that had been left in stalled traffic and brought the supplies back to the Homestead. Later on, as we got more survivors, we did more with training and finding supplies. Sometimes, there are literally rail cars full of food that were left on the train tracks...

Then there's living what's wild and free. In the woods, I can probably name you six or seven nuts found in the Kentucky hills alone. Wild berries, cat tails... asparagus in the spring time... not to mention all the animals that people normally wouldn't eat. I don't know how many of you have tried rabbit or squirrel, but I grew up on it. With a group our size, we'd out hunt everything in the area, so we declared open warfare on the wild hogs roaming the farm fields. We eat pork with almost every meal, and there is a lot of it.

I do regret we had to stop Mr. Davis, and the loss of life of his men, and I will admit, it was me and not Sandra or Mr. Silverman there,"

"Blake," Sandra said, almost tearing his hand off, her grip was so tight.

"But I did not think he was a legitimate person. First off, it is starving times for a lot of people," Blake said and got nods from all around the table, "I'm not into fat shaming, but look at me. I eat well, probably better than most if truth be told... I'm still about fifteen pounds thinner than I've ever been. Mr. Davis on the other hand, reminded me immediately of Jefferson Davis Hogg, and not just because of similar names," Blake paused to take a sip of water and remove his left hand from Sandra's grip before she tore him apart.

His eyes saw Commander Cates gaze and the half smirk on her face, "and, other than Sgt. Silverman here, most of his men were bully-boy thugs. He didn't have anything resembling a normal looking military force. Heck, his men didn't even have on the same uniforms, equipment—"

"I was working with what I was given," Davis thundered, standing up so quickly his chair went flying behind him, "I was given an order by the President of the United States of—"

"Sit down and shut up," Justice Roberts said, his voice overwhelming Davis, "And let him finish his side. Then we can have a discussion, if things remain civil."

"As I was saying," Blake said, taking another sip, "He didn't look credible. It was after he made threats and we took out his Humvee that we talked with Sgt. Silverman and found out, at least according to them, that they were legit. They'd also brought a refrigerated trailer with them, probably to transport stolen food goods, and it was full of slaughtered beef and pigs. He said it was part of the redistribution of foods and had come from the farms. I'd love for Sgt. Silverman to tell you about that, because he was in fact there for part of those raids... so I sent the bully packing to cry in Greenville.

But... He sent men against us. We've been training, both military and civilian. Again, these weren't regular troops he sent against us and, if you are coming to peacefully talk or take inventory as he claimed, why did he send what he thought would be an overwhelming force?"

"Were they killed?" Major Roberts asked.

"To a man Sir," Blake said and winced as Sandra grabbed his hand again, "Well, actually we let one go. He told us where they were all at. I think it was that time... was it that time, Honey?" Blake asked.

"Wait, there was more than one time?" Sola asked.

"Yes, Sir The next time he sent a sniper team, to murder my pregnant wife here. Then it was APCs... and the final time was a small commando unit who shot my wife up full of tranquilizer and was in the process of kidnapping her when we stopped and killed them. All so Mr. Davis could force me to be arrested and our people scattered into the cities. Probably to die starving like the rest of his folks."

"Did you offer to share any of the food?" Commander Cates asked.

"At their first meeting with us? I didn't have any to share. I did tell him if he could help me with some mechanics that maybe we could get some old farm equipment up and running before what had already been planted rotted away in farms all across the valley," Blake told her, "As it was, that's exactly what we ended up doing with Sgt. Silverman."

"That's after you blew up my command post and tried to assassinate me, playing those stupid rock and roll songs on your loud speakers." Davis was livid, his color turning almost a purple.

"Is that true?" Commander Roberts asked.

"Yes Sir, that's when I wasn't getting attacked, snipered at, trying to save my wife from a kidnapping or worrying where this rat was going to attack next. I can't help people out when I'm fighting for my life. I didn't think he was legit at first, but even his own men left him. Sir, I'd really like to say this and then I'm done…

"I didn't believe he was legit at first. I was wrong. He was, and I was the one who made the decision that led to the escalation after our first meeting. If he was the top man, the representative of what the government I personally had thought crumbled into the ashes… Then I wanted no part of that government. My only regret in shelling him was that he wasn't killed in the attack. I gave those orders, Sirs and Ma'am."

Sandra was shaking visibly, her grip almost crushing.

"One last question Mr. Jackson, and then you can save what's left of your hand," Commander Cates said, "you mentioned that the people would be scattered to the cities to starve to death. What did you mean?"

"The cities are death traps, from what I'm hearing. There are no good places to hunt, fish, get clean water or grow food. What are those people in the cities doing? The ones that aren't scraped up and put to work in a FEMA camp? Our folks at the Homestead are all working together. To learn, to work as a community and to survive."

"They're all a bunch of gun nut, military freaks!" Davis exploded.

"Last warning Governor," Lt. Commander Sola said, "Or I'll have you escorted out of here. Sit down and shut up."

"You can't do that! I'm the Governor of the State of Kentucky, appointed by the President of the United States of America. I command the National Guard for the state. I'm the one in charge! I—"

The woman who'd been sitting beside him stood and smacked him so hard it turned his head. She got up and marched to the door, knocked to get the door open, and left.

"What was that about?" Blake asked Sandra,

not realizing that the room had gone deathly silent.

"It appears to be another defection," Sgt. Silverman said, drawing the attention of everyone there.

"Sgt. Silverman. Would you like to speak on your behalf?" Commander Cates said.

"Yes Ma'am. I won't go over everything Mr. Blake there said, because that's how it happened. I left because I did not feel the leadership was following the course of the constitution that I'd sworn to uphold and protect."

"How do you figure?" Davis snarled, still standing.

"I figure, SIR," turning to face Davis and making "Sir" sound like an insult, "Because you were going in and having us ransack farms and people who had prepared for something like this."

"They were right wing conspiracy nuts! All of them had huge armories of weapons and supplies, which the executive order made illegal..." Davis droned on for a few and missed the fact that Silverman was using his index figure to draw circles in the air by his temple.

That made the group chuckle and halted the words from Davis.

"When you go into a farm, you don't take all the livestock. He had us butcher two milk cows, he had us butcher a sow that was ready to give birth to piglets. One of his mercenary buddies shot their livestock guardian dog—"

"He was going to attack my men—"

"You were murdering his family by stealing

their food. Now any animal they had left, if any, would die by the coyotes!" Sgt. Silverman boomed, his voice louder than anybody's in the room.

He sucked in a deep breath, his chest puffing out, looking like he was hulking up to go after Davis.

"Gentlemen," Commander Cates said, calming them, "Go on Sgt. Silverman."

"Yes Ma'am. If you kill off a farmers breeding stock, how's he going to continue to farm them? You use a resource like that over and over until you breed more breeders. You eat the babies—"

"Yes, I'm familiar with the concept," Cates said.

"And the men he had working with us. Dregs. I think he emptied a jail out, handed them guns and told them to march. That's how poor quality the mercenaries were. I was not out with every food gathering, but I went along with the one where the dog was killed. I had to really think hard, and when I had guns that Mr. and Mrs. Jackson's group held on me, in my eyes, I realized right then that I was becoming a part of the problem, not a part of the solution. I admit, I deserted my duty, Ma'am and Sirs. I did not however, kill any of the men that were sent after us. Those probably defected as well."

"You feel that Mr. Davis was not acting in a lawful manner according to his office, and the trust placed in him by the President of the United States?" Justice Roberts asked, raising one eyebrow.

"No Sir, not at all."

Sandra raised her hand, as if she was in school.

THE WORLD COWERS

All eyes turned towards her and she stood, waiting for the others to take their seats. She was used to people ignoring her because of her small, slender size and elfin features.

"I too, was a commissioned officer at one time. In all my years, I was told that you can never get in trouble for following orders, unless you were following illegal ones. In this case, not only what Mr. Davis was doing was unconstitutional, but it goes against our basic rights as human beings."

"I followed the constitution, I was not breaking the law! I am the law—"

"That's enough Mr. Davis! Private First Class Sherman!" Cates yelled.

Sandra pushed her chair back and faced John Davis, while Martin Cates looked on, eyes wide. It was nothing like any trial he'd ever sat in on.

"You want to know what else about Mr. Davis? We've got some of his men, they grouped up with us just last week. He's abusing his authority to gain sexual favors from the women staffers and soldiers, and us "right wing conspiracy gun nuts" don't have half the food hoard that Boss Hogg here has—"

Davis let out a strangled cry and rushed Sandra. Both Silverman and Blake jumped up in alarm, but Sandra was poetry in motion. She'd not lied and the information was accurate, but she knew Davis was at his breaking point and had deliberately held off to show the panel how out of control and unfit he was. Davis attacking a pregnant woman was not something that anyone but Sandra had predicted.

He didn't try to box her, instead he acted like he was going to bum rush her and use his weight to ride her to the ground. Sandra stepped back and delivered a fast chop to the big man's throat, being careful not to crush his windpipe. A choking and sputtering Davis crashed into Blake and Blake's chair, spilling Blake into Silverman who also stumbled, hitting the ground.

Somehow, the big man was up first, and a cursing Blake tried to grab him, but Sandra was already moving out of his reach to give herself some distance.

"I'll fucking kill—" Davis started to say when Sandra snapped a kick into his head, and then used a spinning heel kick to knock him off his feet.

That was the exact moment that the electronic lock clicked open and PFC Sherman opened the door behind Sandra. It wasn't his fault, because in a fight things happen so fast, a second is all it takes for a quick action or countermove. Sometimes a lot less. Sherman had gotten inside there as fast as he could, and he saw Governor Davis on his knees coughing and trying to get to his feet. He was reaching for his pistol when he saw Sandra deliver a crushing knee to the Governor's face.

He pulled his gun and leveled it at the base of Sandra's skull.

"Stand down, son," Sola barked, the whole room now on their feet.

"Sir, the Governor—"

"Stand down son, before I bury you under the

brig," the man's words were said so low and in a growl, that Sherman broke eye contact with Sandra to see the expression on the man's face.

He swallowed and holstered his weapon.

"Please get Mr. Davis here medical attention as needed, and then report back to me." Commander Cates said, her voice high and surprised.

"Yes Ma'am," Sherman said, trying to pull the Governor to his feet and not succeeding.

"I'm the Governor of the—" Davis sputtered.

"Oh shut up," Justice Stevens told him.

They watched as the Governor struggled to his feet, threating vile things to everyone there. The man who'd stood to speak for him eventually had to help get the man to his feet and the three of them left.

"Now," Cates said looking at them, "Since you've admitted your guilt in this matter—"

"Ma'am," Sandra bolted upright, interrupting, "I can't let these men take the—"

"Sit down, Mrs. Jackson. I've had enough interruptions for the day. Since guilt has been admitted by the parties involved, I'd like to deliberate with the panel here. Wait here for your escort back to your holding cells."

"We're in the shit now," Silverman said, watching the five of them get up and leave the room.

"Can we get out?" Blake asked when they had all left.

"Locked," Silverman said checking.

"Why did you do it?" Sandra asked Blake, her

words angry.

"What?" Blake asked, never before having been the object of her fury.

"Take the blame for me."

Blake looked at his hand and realized that she'd been trying to warn him off, and not that she was nervous.

"Because you're my wife and you're carrying my baby. Chris is my buddy, but you're his momma."

CHAPTER 6

"Damnit Miranda, listen to this." Martin Cates held the handset up so his wife could listen into Rebel radio.

She'd been reading old case files from when she'd studied law herself, but this wasn't a situation that was handled in any law books or any Supreme Court cases she'd studied. She'd met Martin years earlier when she was studying for the bar, they'd fallen in love, married and, when she decided to pursue a career in the military, he'd been supportive. Now, he was a pain in her side, especially regarding the Jackson issue.

Maybe it was that she wanted him to shut up about it, but she relented and took the handset and walked towards the entrance of the DUMB so she could get better reception. She knew she could have gone into the communications room and dialed in, but she wanted distance from her husband to think.

"I'll listen, just give me some space," she told her husband, who'd largely gone forgotten in the hearing and was embarrassed that he didn't do anything to shield the pregnant woman from Davis's charge.

"Ok, I'll be here." Cates watched as his wife walked away, then sat down at the folding table, one of the Spartan furnishings in their shared room.

He'd been going stir crazy living underground for months, eating the same canned food, jogging loops through the inner tunnels for exercise. Then he'd overheard some of the communications guys talking about Rebel Radio. The name alone got him curious and he asked. Apparently there was a guy who gave survival tips on a frequency and it'd become one of their favorite pastimes. He had a handset in the locker, so he tuned in at the appointed time and became a fan immediately.

He couldn't broadcast with his handset, but he could listen to information that had been shared all over the country. It wasn't the most reliable information, sometimes passing through two or more people's mouths and interpretations. He heard some big whoppers and outright falsehoods repeated enough times it made his head spin!

The thing that had alarmed him enough to get his wife involved finally, was listening to the tone of the country now calling in on the frequency and how it seemed an uprising was going to happen. Martin thought he was a pretty smart guy and, if the word got out that one of the post apocalypse's cult heroes was being held, charged and potentially executed, it would be ugly. He sat and stewed, hoping his wife would come to the same conclusions he did, because he couldn't talk to her about Blake any more. She thought he was blinded by his "fan devotion", whatever that meant.

Their door opened and he stood. His wife's face was grim.

"We have to get him on the radio," she said.

"Why? Has something else happened?"

"They're talking about coming and getting him. Do you know how many people listen to this show?" Miranda asked him.

"I do, that's what I've been telling you."

"Go get the Jacksons. I'll call ahead to Sherman or whoever's on post. Get them up to communications right away. I want them on the air and I want it looped."

"What do you want them to say?" He asked, worried and wanting to hurry to listen in for himself.

"The truth, they are being held, they are safe, they were tried and they are awaiting our decision. I do want you to tell them that this could be bad though, so don't be inflammatory. I don't want more people hurt."

"They won't either," he said, kissing his wife, almost running out the door.

"That's why, despite what's going on, I think they'll do it. God, I need a drink," she told the empty room and sat down, putting her face in her hands.

§ § §

"Pamela, it's safe to assume you're fired," Davis said, furious and venting his anger on his assistant who'd been in her quarters packing. Davis was standing in her open doorway, blocking the only exit.

"I figured as much when I decked you. What happened to your face? Besides me?" Pamela asked, her disdain clear in her voice.

Davis's nose had been splinted and half of his face and neck were already bruising. Only one small amount of that could be attributed to her slap.

"Shut up! Listen you stupid bit—"

Pamela had her back to him but sensed him moving past the door jam, hearing his steps. She spun, pulling a slim knife from her bags, stopping the Governor short as he almost impaled himself on the stiletto's thin blade. His arms had been raised as if to throttle her.

"I no longer work for you. I'll get with Commander Cates and find out when I need to vacate the premises, but if you so much as come any closer…"

"You dare to threaten me? I'm the Governor—"

"Not for long, and not if you don't move out of the lady's room," a voice said.

Pamela couldn't hear who'd spoken as the Governor's bulk was blocking her view, but she heard the distinctive clicks of two safeties being turned off. Davis turned slowly and two guards he didn't recognize were standing there, guns trained on him.

"Like I said," the older one repeated, "If you don't start moving out of the lady's room right now, I'm going to assume your intent was not one of a gentleman, and splatter your fat ass with tumblers. Your move, Governor."

"You can't do this, you work for me!" The governor's voice came out in a hoarse whisper.

"I'm not part of the national guard, and neither is he," he nodded to the second man who raised his rifle up, bringing the Governor in line with his sights.

Either soldier could have hit him without aiming at that distance, but the move was meant to intimidate, and it worked. Immediately Davis dropped his hands to his sides. Pamela as well, lowered her knife, but kept it close to her side, ready to use in an instant. She stepped around Davis and approached the guards. The younger one moved out of the way and she slipped out of the doorway.

"Governor Davis, you've received a message in communications. When we couldn't find you in your rooms as ordered, even after you were in medical, we came to find you. You know how bad this looks, Sir?"

"I run this state!" Davis fumed, but he was losing steam.

"Sir, you need to come with us," the younger soldier said, taking two steps closer, rifle still raised.

BOYD CRAVEN

"Do I get cuffed?" Davis squeaked.

"It's up to you, Sir. If you make one more hostile or threatening move, I have no problem ending you."

"I'll come." Davis said meekly, realizing for the first time how deep the hole he had dug was.

§ § §

"He did what?" Lt. Commander Sola demanded, as the soldiers walked Governor John Davis in at gunpoint.

"I didn't do anything! I was having a conversation with my personal assistant, she and I—"

"She pulled a knife and was about to pig stick him, when he charged her. Looked like he was going to choke her Sir," the younger soldier answered.

"You Sir, are an idiot," Lt. Commander Sola said. "These two would have splattered you all across the room if you would have touched her."

"That's what I told him Sir," the holder soldier said.

"You two, take positions outside the door with the Governor. I have to make a report of this," he said, over the Governor's objections and threats.

"You two are going to regret this," the Governor spat as they held him outside communications.

"Sir, I follow orders. You are not in my chain of command. I may have to respect your office, but I do not have to respect you, Sir. Threats are not something you have the ability to follow through,

64

so how about you shut up before I let that pregnant lady beat your ass again?" The older soldier, Collins, growled.

"You... How?" Davis stuttered.

"Oh yeah," the younger soldier agreed, "The whole base has heard about it now. How the fat sack of shit, Boss Hogg got his ass handed to him by a petite pregnant lady. I can't wait to hear if this is on Rebel Radio later on!"

"No need to rile him up," Collins said.

The door opened and Davis was asked to join them inside.

§ § §

"Tank," Sandra asked, "What was Davis doing in there?"

They had passed the big man being escorted out by two grizzled soldiers, both of whom were almost as red in the face as the man they held their guns on.

"I'm not sure Ma'am, I was just asked to bring you here to communications."

"But why?" Blake asked.

"Commander's orders."

CHAPTER 7

Sgt. Smith had started breaking down camp. It was the second day after Blake and Sandra had been arrested and taken. Almost everyone of the men that came with him were going back. They'd talked and even fought over it. In the end, the units decided to stick together. There were a few holdouts, but they would soon be leaving the Homestead, so they wouldn't bring trouble to the doorstep of the big extended family. Many of the men who would be joining them were also packing up, hugging their families goodbye, perhaps for the last time.

"How many will be left here?" Duncan asked.

He'd been put on medical restriction again by Lisa and Martha. He'd had a weakness in his left side and Martha speculated that he'd had a mild heart attack. It had been both shocking and sobering, so he rested in the living room where he could be close to the base radio and where the core group of the Homestead congregated so he could still be a part of it.

"Quite a bit. With the food we're going to be sending them, we'll have enough food to still last the winter and then some. The corn and soybean crop that got harvested is going to be sent along as barter/payment for the men who don't have equipment, uniforms," Bobby, his son-in-law told him. "About 100 people all told."

"Half of the Homestead is going to be leaving?" Lisa asked, her voice shocked.

"Yeah, and the thing is, about half of those that are leaving are volunteers. Single men and women. We won't be hurting for defense as long as Sandra's squad can maintain training for everyone over the age of ten." Bobby finished, putting a pencil up he'd been using to doodle on the notebook he had.

"Any word from Blake or Sandra?" Melissa asked, Bobby's fiancée, and a member of Sandra's squad.

Duncan winced, "No, but I don't expect to hear anything right away. I'm happier not to be hearing from Boss Hogg though. If I heard his smug voice over the radio, I'd know it'd be over for them."

"Me too baby," Lisa said, sending Chris over with a plate of cookies.

"I can't eat these," Duncan said, sounding sad.

"Grandma said you can. Here," Chris picked

one up and tried shoving it into Duncan's mouth.

"No, no, I got this," he said, making the recliner he'd been leaned back in sit up straight.

He nibbled on the cookie and looked around, "I fell asleep last night. How was Rebel Radio?" Duncan asked.

"With Blake off, everyone used the time to uh…" Patty said and her words trailed off.

"Yeah?" Duncan asked.

"Well you see… with Blake and Sandra arrested, things are looking ugly…" David told him.

"How ugly?" Duncan asked, getting frustrated.

"They're forming a militia to free them or avenge them," Bobby finished, "and they're not being quiet or subtle about it. If people knew where they were being held—"

"They'd do the same thing we would, go and get them." Duncan said, finishing the thought.

"They're family," Lisa told the room.

"How long until Rebel Radio tonight?" Duncan asked, having slept off and on for quite a bit.

"Blake's time is on in an hour, but people are chattering away already," David said, changing the *frequency and turning it on.*

"*…government thinks they can push us around, what they did to Blake and Sandra is one example of the reason things got so out of whack….*"

"*I hear ya, after that bozo tried raiding Blake's Homestead…*"

"Wow," Duncan said, is it been like this?"

"Ever since Davis got on the horn a couple days

ago and those two were arrested. They have to do something about it sooner or—"

The feed was interrupted by somebody with a strong signal. It came in loud and clear on the base unit at the Homestead and R.E.M.'s song "*It's The End Of The World As We Know It*" blasted out.

"What's this?" Duncan asked.

"Somebody got ahold of a good song at least," Lisa said, smiling and sang along.

Her voice was joined in by the others who were not lost in the irony of the situation and, when the song cut off, everyone almost fell out of their chair as the person spoke.

"*Good afternoon everyone, this is Back Country J, Blake Jackson here with my wife Sandra,*"

"*Hi, it's Sandra,*" her voice piped up, "*We're talking to you from an undisclosed government facility where we've been charged with multiple counts of murder and treason. I'm sorry I'm not on during my normal hours, but I've been told they'll play this message once an hour on a loop, so everyone gets a chance to hear from us.*

We are fine, we've been treated well and by no means do we want people going off half-cocked. At this time, Governor Davis has been relieved of his duties and Sandra and I are awaiting the court's decision."

"It's military grade," Patty said, looking at the controls and was shushed by everyone.

"*I want you all to know, no matter what it is the court decides, I will go with and abide by their deci-*

sion. *I debated this very issue on the air with you all, and I stand by my convictions. A government that would steal from the people and bully us around isn't one I'm going to suffer. Wow, you guys let me say that?"* Blake said quietly to somebody wherever he was talking too.

"Anyways, it was my choice, my decision and it does in fact look like remnants of our government are coming out of hiding to start the rebuilding process and fight the invasion that's coming in through the Southwestern border of the US.

"So with that, I'm told I'll be able to come on the air when our hearing is done and give everyone the verdict. I was given the option of being allowed to do this, because the people here don't want to see anybody else hurt. I don't either. This is Blake and Sandra, and we'll talk to you soon."

"Bubye," Sandra said, her voice bubbling.

§ § §

"Cue the iPod," Blake told the man sitting to his left and waited until it was his time to speak.

"Good afternoon everyone, this is Back Country J, Blake Jackson here with my wife Sandra," he said grinning and handing the mic over to her.

"Hi, it's Sandra," Sandra said, giving the mic back to Blake.

"Talking to you from an undisclosed government facility where we've been charged with multiple counts of murder and treason. I'm sorry I'm not on during my normal hours, but I've been told they'll play this message once an hour on a loops so everyone gets a chance to hear from us.

We are fine, we've been treated well and by no means do we want people going off halfcocked. At this time, Governor Davis has been relieved of his duties and Sandra and I are awaiting the court's decision."

Blake paused to get a sip of water. He'd been eager and ready to make this transmission, especially when he'd gotten the news about Davis.

"I want you all to know, no matter what it is the court decides, I will go with and abide by their decision. I debated this very issue on the air with you all, and I stand by my convictions. A government that would steal from the people and bully us around isn't one I'm going to suffer." He forgot to let off the transmit switch and turned to Cates in amusement.

Cates sat there, his arms folded, "Wow, you guys let me say that?" Blake said before continuing, "Anyways, it was my choice, my decision and it does in fact look like remnants of our government are coming out of hiding to start the rebuilding process and fight the invasion that's coming in through the southwestern border of the US.

"So with that, I'm told I'll be able to come on the air when our hearing is done and give everyone the verdict. I was given the option of being allowed to do this, because the people here don't want to see anybody else hurt. I don't either. This is Blake and

71

Sandra, and we'll talk to you soon."

"Bubye," Sandra said, her voice bubbling.

Blake cut off the mic and handed it over to the communications officer.

"Was that ok?" Blake asked, turning to look Cates in the eye.

"Yeah, I think that'll go a long way to calm things down. There's already been enough rotten apples in NATO and our own government, and I don't want the people just declaring open season on the good guys that are actually trying to help. It'd be counterproductive to everything we are trying to do here."

"Come on folks," PFC Sherman said, "I have to wrap this up and put you back in your cells."

"They really booted Davis?" Sandra asked.

"Yeah, they kicked your interview up the chain of command. The President was still going to keep him, until several women came forward and confirmed your story, Sandra. Then he almost attacked his assistant not a few seconds before his escorts showed up. The President had his hands tied and now he's looking to appoint a new one."

"Anybody in particular?" Sandra asked.

"No, probably another political crony. Hopefully the new guy isn't as bad as Davis was," Martin told them.

"I'd like to have seen Davis's face when he got that news!" Blake said, excited.

"The President called Davis himself!" Martin's voice was high pitched and Blake swore the word himself sounded like hisself.

"So what happens now?" Sandra asked.

"You're still awaiting the verdict. My wife is tight lipped, and hates that I involved myself in this case."

"Hey, thanks," Sandra said, pausing to give him a hug, "but you don't work on making your wife angry. You know what they say, happy wife, happy house."

"True," Blake said, taking her and starting to walk again after Sherman made an exasperated sound.

"I'll be back for you tomorrow. In the meantime, keep yourselves out of trouble," Cates said, giving them a little wave and took a different corridor away from them.

"Bye," they both chorused and then laughed.

"Tank, you look like somebody pinched you, what is it?" Sandra asked after they'd walked a few more minutes, pausing at the door.

"Somebody's waiting inside, I just caught a glimpse through the door," he said, using the keycard with his free hand, his other holding his pistol at the ready.

Blake opened the door and was the first one in, "Lucy, I'm home," he said, trying to be goofy.

"That sounds funny coming out of a hillbilly's mouth," Franklin Hines said, turning and standing.

"Sir, I didn't know you were going to be down here." Sherman told him, pointing to their cells.

Blake and Sandra went in, never offering Sher-

BOYD CRAVEN

man any problems, and put their hands through the bars to get their cuffs removed. Sherman did that and then remained inside the room, something he usually didn't do.

"You got somewhere else to be?" Hines asked, looking at the soldier.

"No Sir, I'm here to guard the prisoners, Sir," Sherman said.

"Tank, go on man," Silverman said, getting up from the cot where he'd been laying down.

"Sgt. Silverman?" he asked.

"You weren't taking the hint. I think Mr. Hines here wants to talk to us. Without little ears," Silverman finished.

Blake and Sandra smiled at the reference, using that very same wording when wanting to discuss things without Chris overhearing them.

"I uh… Yes, no problem. I'll be on the other side of the door, Mr. Hines. Just knock and I'll let you out."

"Thank you," Hines said, watching him leave and then waiting for the electronic lock to click shut.

"So…" Sandra started.

Hines grabbed a folding chair and brought it closer to the bars of their cell and sat down, the metal of the seat making popping sounds.

"So I'm guessing you heard about Davis?" Hines asked.

"Yeah," Blake said, "I heard he threw a fit."

"More like a conniption," Sandra added.

THE WORLD COWERS

"Wait, I haven't heard… Fill an old soldier in," Silverman said in protest.

"John Davis was relieved of his position by POTUS a little while ago. We'd heard rumors from outsiders, but figured it was all a part of the whole "it's the government's fault,"" he said making air quotes, "We'd been listening to your broadcasts before Davis involved himself in your affairs. You guys seemed like pretty level-headed, honest Christians. Working for the governor directly, I couldn't believe it when he came back ranting and raving."

"Yeah, that was funny," Silverman said, "but I want to know, did he cry? Did he have a heart attack?"

"Not quite, he was livid and trying to order everybody around until Lt. Commander Sola reminded him that he was above his pay grade and he only commanded the National Guard. That was it. He'd lost that. I don't think he took the rejection well."

"So is he still here?" Blake and Sandra asked.

"Yeah, they're confining him to quarters until the trial is over with. They're afraid if they stuck him in that empty cell there between Blake and Sgt. Silverman…"

They all grinned at that.

"So is he now going to stand trial? I mean, what he did—"

"Most of what was needed to be said or found out has been already done now. I won't mind a new boss, let me tell you. Until I do, I report to the President directly, and that guy scared me when they first selected him. Anyways, I wanted to make sure you guys know that. That's not the reason I'm here though," Hines said, shifting his weight back and crossing his legs.

"What are you here for?" Sandra asked him.

"I'd like to pick your brain on something I heard in the meeting, and go into more depth and detail. It's actually to help me do my job better, it's got nothing to do with the trial. You don't have to answer me, and I'd understand if you told me to bug off," he finished and lapsed into silence.

Blake thought about it and nodded, "I don't mind helping," he told Hines.

"Good, I was hoping so. Your community, the Homestead, is further ahead than any other group. The sheer size and self-sustainability is amazing. The only groups of any size like that or larger are the groups we've been trying to feed at the camps or the centers in the city. What struck me during the trial was how you said everyone works, everyone helps and everyone eats. How can you do that? I'm assuming you don't have two hundred beds in the farm, do you?"

Sandra giggled and Blake smiled, "No, other than those of us who live in the house, the barn's loft has been converted into living quarters. Hammocks and rope beds with whatever we can use for padding and blankets. I believe the term is hot cot?" Blake asked, looking to his wife who nodded, "because with that many people there is enough work to keep people going 24/7/365. We've got some great organizers in our group." Blake said, thinking of Bobby and how Melissa and he had been figuring out the rotation schedules before they'd been taken.

"Ok, that makes sense. Would you say your group acts like a military group or militia?" Hines asked.

"No, not really. We encourage everyone to participate in learning survival skills, to shoot… I'm even learning a ton of new tricks and I grew up in the woods practically. Then there is the school sessions we set up for the kids."

Hines eyebrows rose, "Oh? School? It's almost fall, how did you manage that? You have teachers?"

"Yes," Sandra answered, "quite a few now. Without recess or excessive walking to and from classes, school has been working out quite well. Besides, if you kept all those kids locked up with no structure, they'd drive everyone around them insane."

"How can you do that with that many people… er… kids?" Hines asked.

"It isn't that bad," Blake answered, "My father in law and I take the kids out for an hour or two nature walk where we teach them about foraging. While we're out there, we're putting their energy and hands to use in picking nuts and berries and teaching them the basics of trapping and hunting. It's really a win win. Instead of recess, they help out and they learn a ton. That's just one type of learning besides math, history and reading."

"What about their reading levels?" Hines asked.

"You'd be surprised about this," Sandra told him, "we have a ton of kids that said they felt lost without their Ipods and electronics. Now that none of it is working, the older kids have taken up reading. I got lucky, when I met Blake we went to a storage auction. We got a few boxes of books in addition to what Blake already had or we found in our scavenging missions. Now the older kids are helping the few teachers we have to teach the younger kids to read. Can you imagine what the world would have been like if the TV was never invented?" Sandra said, her voice excited.

"I've had the same issues with my daughter," Hines admitted, "but I never thought the lights going out would increase literacy."

"It's not a perfect place, don't get me wrong," Blake told him, "With close quarters, there's no privacy, there's arguments and hurt feelings. We kind of run things with big town hall type meetings."

"So there's no set leader?"

"No," Blake said.

"Yes," Silverman and Sandra said in the same moment.

Blake looked at first one and then the other then back to Hines.

"I guess there is, but I never wanted it," Blake admitted.

"So is it run democratically?" Hines asked.

"Where are you going with this, Sir?" Silverman asked.

"The thing is, we've got more people than we

can care for—"

"We can't just take in a ton of people at once," Blake told him, putting his hands up in a stopping motion, "Besides, we're locked up and I doubt the Homestead will do much cooperation with anybody at this point. We're still waiting to find out if we're getting fitted for nooses."

"No, don't worry about a hanging. Firing squad either. I can't talk about things related to that, but what I was going to ask, is if let's say you had five thousand people to take care of—"

"No," Blake said.

"Hear me out. I have five thousand people in this one camp. We send food in, and we're getting very little out as in terms of the components we're building for the electrical stations or the power line equipment. I don't know what half of it is, but a lot of the parts, or tools to build the parts, need to be handmade. That's what they're doing. It's an enormous drain of resources for very little output. Now the cities… The gang violence in the cities is horrendous. People are forming their own gangs for protection. It's bad, and the last big food distribution in Greenville, there were riots and more fires."

"What do the people do in the cities?" Blake asked.

"Do what they can to survive, wait for the next food shipments. Stuff like that. But you brought up a very good point in the meetings. Cities don't make sense right now. There's no food, no way to get it or produce it there, and the water is less than potable. It's a cesspool, basically."

"That's gross," Sandra told him and he nodded.

"What's worse, is the people don't want to be relocated to the camps."

"Well, can you blame them?" Blake asked, "We've all heard the horror stories about what happened in Alabama and the breakout in Louisiana. Heck, I talked to a boy over the radio that was in one of those camps. He was held prisoner and the families were separated. Men in one building, women in another, the kids separated, and they very rarely got to visit with each other. That's jail. That isn't helping them out."

"Yes, I know. You must understand, those facilities were run by some NATO officers from countries where conditions are much harsher than we Americans are used to. Some speak our language, some don't. You strip away the humanity of people and you get people at their best or worst. Are you guys familiar with the Stanford Prison Experiment?" Hines asked.

"Yeah." Sandra replied, surprising Blake, who was looking at him with a blank expression.

"Yeah, I have," Silverman said, "It's the ones where volunteers were asked to play the roles of prisoners and guards. They really got into the roles and they had to break the experiment off early before permanent damage was done."

"Yes, exactly," Hines said, "That's what we have here, on a much larger scale. Other than the Governor, I'm the second Warden, so to speak. I'd like to hear your thoughts on this."

"Why hold them there? Inside the camps?" Blake asked.

"Excuse me?"

"Aren't most of these camps in out of the way places, away from the bigger cities mostly?" Blake asked.

"Sometimes outside of a major area yes, but yeah, they are out of the way usually. Why?"

"Well, here's a novel thought. How hard would it be to start asking for volunteers from the cities to settle around the camp areas, and open the camps up. No more prisoners, no more forced labor. If they want to eat, they work. If they don't, well, they go hungry or find their own food." Blake told him.

"That's along the lines of what I was thinking as well. It's not something the President has agreed to at this point."

"But why not let them go free if they choose? Maybe they have a family farm or ranch they can return to. I think the biggest mistake was rounding people up until the camps were full with no end goal in mind." Blake said, the idea of the camps making him furious.

"And those who want to stay, stay?"

"Yes," Sandra answered.

"That's what I'd run past the Governor and President as well. That whole fiasco in Alabama was horrible, and the civil unrest it generated when the stories got out," he pointed to Blake, "no thanks to a hillbilly with a radio…"

"Hey now, we just had a big reach with that antenna, we just relayed messages," Blake said.

"Sometimes inflammatory messages." Hines said, not backing down.

"What's your point?" Sandra asked, annoyance in her voice.

"The point is, there are people around the country that are looking to model your group as the way to go forward for the rebuilding. I just wanted to pick your brain a bit…"

There was a knock on the door, and then it clicked open. Hines stood and PFC Sherman walked in, followed by Mr. and Mrs. Cates, Justice Stevens and the rest of the panel of five.

"We were told we'd find you here, Mr. Hines." Commander Cates said, her voice frosty.

"Yes. What can I do for you?" he asked, puzzled at her frown and the looks he was getting from the others.

Blake started to sweat. The entire panel was there, and four out of five looked pissed off.

"What were you discussing?" Justice Stevens asked, "We weren't supposed to be discussing anything with the prisoners."

"Oh, I wasn't. I was finding out how the Homestead worked. The basics. The cities are going to shit… Ooops, pardon my language, and something Blake said in the meeting made me think that perhaps we should be rebuilding in the suburbs or even small towns. It'll put people further apart, but I don't think keeping people in a concrete jungle is going to be the solution."

"Oh, so you weren't talking to him about the decision?" Commander Cates asked.

"Wait, you already made a decision? When?" Martin asked his wife, the shock evident on his face...

"This morning at breakfast. We just got word from the President, and he has accepted our findings and told us to proceed. The thing with Davis delayed proceedings. We just got out of communications." Miranda Cates answered.

Sandra put her hands through the bars, taking Blake's.

"Director Hines, you want to tell them?" Cates asked.

Martin shot his wife a look that conveyed how betrayed he felt.

Franklin Hines nodded, "Sure. You two were convicted of all charges," he said looking at Blake and Sandra.

CHAPTER 8

"Duncan, you sit down!" Lisa berated her husband.

It had been two days of thunderous silence since Blake's last transmission, and everyone had feared the worst. The volunteers and military personal, former and present, were packed and were going to leave in a convoy the following morning. Duncan had insisted on getting out of the house to help, but he was still weak and both Lisa and Martha had feared the stress and anxiety was going to be the literal death of him.

"I'm going, just help me get my shoes on," he said, his face bathed in sweat.

His chest was hurting again, but he hadn't wanted to say anything. If it was to be his last day on earth, he wanted a moment to say goodbye to the group of volunteers and families that had thrown in with them through thick and thin.

"We can get him to the porch swing," Martha said, trying to placate him.

"That'll be fine for me," Duncan said, chafing at the rest.

"Uhhh… Guys?" David said, pulling the headphones off, "tell everybody to turn on Rebel Radio, five minutes."

"Who was it?" Lisa asked, one shoulder under Duncan's, as she'd been trying to guide him back to a chair.

"Pamela Wisemer, assistant to the Governor. She said all units at the Homestead, and from Silverman's camp especially, to tune in."

"I don't know if I can listen to this," Duncan said, his legs going rubbery.

They barely got him into the recliner and Lisa saw the gray pallor and ran for the nitro pills they'd found in numerous scavenging trips. It wasn't far, just high up on a shelf in the kitchen where Chris couldn't get it.

"They also said," Patty told them, "That you'll be hearing from Blake and Sandra."

Lisa gave Duncan the nitro and almost immediately it started working as he left it under his tongue. It did nothing to quell the anxiety.

"Did you hear…" Sgt. Smith burst in, the front door almost rebounding back into his face, he'd come in so hard and so fast.

Lisa spun on him and if looks could kill, the

Sargent would be worm food, perhaps even road-kill fed as worm food.

"Sit still, and breathe," Lisa told him, watching the color coming back into his face.

"Get Chris," Duncan said, "one way or another…"

"I'll go get him," Bobby said, running out the door, leaving it hanging open.

"Are you ok?" Lisa asked, kneeling by Duncan's side.

"Yeah, it was close. I think the stress has been getting to me," Duncan admitted.

"One way or another…" Lisa said, but she couldn't continue, she was choking up.

"Hey, here it comes," David said, taking the headphones off and unplugging them, letting the speakers fill the room.

Bobby burst back in the door, carrying a giggling Chris upside down and performed a wrestling move on the couch, bouncing the now laughing boy. They were in time, and once again R.E.M.'s iconic song started to play.

"Do you think…?" Duncan asked the room.

"I'm worried," Lisa said, sitting on the floor in front of her husband.

Chris climbed up into Bobby's lap, while Bobby whispered that they'd be hearing about his parents. Patty took her headphones off, got up and walked towards the kitchen, stretching. She could hear everything well, but she wanted to stand in the doorway and let Sgt. Smith have a place to sit. He walked in and took a seat just as the song was ending.

"*Good afternoon everybody, this is Back Country J, Blake Jackson for another addition of Rebel Radio!*"

Everybody looked at each other, eyes wide.

"*If you won't tell them, I will. Quit playing,*" Sandra's voice said, her tone playful.

"*Ok, ok. Sorry! Anyways,*" Blake said before going on, his voice crystal clear over the radio, "*This isn't your usual Rebel Radio broadcast, obviously. I needed to fill people in, and do so in a quick manner so once things were worked out. This seemed the quickest way, so please bear with me. A trial, or hearing of sorts, took place. I took responsibility for my actions and Sandra and myself were found Guilty. Wait! Don't have heart attack Duncan, it's good news!*"

Everyone looked at Duncan who was red faced. "Blasted kid," he growled before he was hushed by everyone.

"*Everyone who's listened in to the broadcast knows all about John Davis, or Boss Hogg as I called him. The hearing highlighted the fact that he was not in fact running his office as he was supposed to, and the President has removed him. I spoke with the President myself, and the negotiations for our pardons has been met. First thing though, they needed a new Governor, and they needed one now,*"

"Oh God, they made him Governor?" Patty asked.

"Shhhhhhhhhhhhhhhhhhhhhh!" Everyone hissed.

"Talking with the panel and the President, it was decided that Franklin Hines, the director of FEMA will be taking over Mr. Davis's position. Until a replacement is found, I'll be working with Mr. Hines in his former role. I have no wish to work here any longer than necessary, but Chris, Duncan, Lisa; we'll be coming home soon."

Everyone erupted in cheers.

"For me, this means a lot of travel and transport. I would like nothing more than to have our own people work with me as I travel, so Sandra's squad, get ready to roll, also one unit of Sgt. Smith's as well."

"What about Sandra?" a voice cut into the transmission, and everyone blinked, wondering who it was.

"That sounds like Z," Patty whispered.

"Hey, is that Miss Z?" Blake asked.

"Yeah, uh... sorry. Hi."

"Well, I'm glad you asked. For now, the remaining folks at the Homestead need to get ready. We're going to be hosting a bit of a party soon, and Sandra is going to be in charge! There's a lot I cannot say over the open air, nor do I even want to go to scramble to discuss it, just know that I'll be home to tell my family in person, and for those of you who aren't at the Homestead... Get on up here. Kentucky will never be the same again, and make sure you listen in, because the new Governor Hines is going to be asking a lot of us in the coming months. I have a Huey to catch, so this is Black Jackson," he said *"and this is Sandra,"* she said, *"signing off for now,"* they both chorused.

THE WORLD COWERS

The music queued back up, and everyone sat and listened to it in mute silence before Patty launched herself towards the Radio stand, trying to pick up the mic before they had walked away. She'd tripped over her own foot in her haste and at the last second, Sgt. Smith braced himself as her whole body weight collided with him, knocking them both to the ground. They came to rest, arms and legs tangled up, both trying to separate quickly. Patty made it to her feet first and grabbed the mic.

"Blake? Sandra? You still there, come in over?" Patty said, taking her finger off the mic key.

"*Just barely,*" Sandra said, her voice quiet.

"You take care of yourself and that baby!"

"*You're talking about Blake, aren't you?*" Sandra asked, laughing.

"Yeah, him too," Patty said, smiling so big it made her cheeks hurt.

"*I promise. See you in an hour, Sandra and Blake out.*"

§ § §

Two helicopters landed an hour later; the Huey brought the Jacksons back home with some men the Homesteaders didn't recognize, some in uniform, some not, the second was an Apache, which also landed. It'd been their escort apparently.

"Dad! Mom!" Chris shouted, running towards them, his eyes watering from the dust kicked up from the rotor wash.

Both Jacksons broke into a run and when Chris was no more than eight feet away he leapt, effectively tackling Blake. Sandra laughed as two of her men rolled on the ground, wrestling and hugging. The pain that Blake felt from his healed gunshot wounds didn't slow him much.

Duncan and Lisa waited on the porch swing while the rest of the Homestead surrounded the small group, shouting questions. As was the custom, Blake and Sandra led everyone towards the house, where they could sit on the steps and talk to more people at once. Many of the security forgot their places and left their concealment, shocking some of the men and women traveling with Blake and Sandra, but the whole Homestead had a sense of carnival in the air. For many people there, the couple had been their saviors, saving them from horrible fates or starvation. Blake and Sandra were not just the head of the Homestead, they were beloved property of the people.

"Would you look at that?" Sgt. Smith said, standing next to Duncan.

"I'm going to have to talk to them about breaking ranks and keeping their eyes on their jobs," Duncan growled.

"Go easy old man," Sgt. Smith said, "you don't want to pop a blood vessel now."

"I'll pop your—"

"I'll just have Patty tackle you down old man, don't you sass me," Sgt. Smith said grinning and turned to see the normally silent woman turn a dark red color in the face.

"Not everyone broke ranks," Duncan said, "I don't see Corrine."

"She's a crafty one," David said, walking out, letting the last of the sun's dying rays to blind him, smiling deeply.

The former slaver felt as if a big weight had been lifted from his chest. Although Blake hadn't saved him directly, he'd been the one to allow David to redeem himself for not being strong enough to have walked away from his brother's evil plans. Blake was also the one who'd figured out that, even though David had lived in a nest of vipers, he was the one that had done all he could for the women he was in charge of. With Blake back, David once again felt like he belonged.

"Oh really?" Corrine said, walking around the porch, startling David so badly, he almost fell off the side of the porch, over the railing.

"Oh my God, woman..." David blurted, red in the face from embarrassment.

"Let's go see them," she said, motioning for him to come down.

Together, hand in hand they walked to the group, not waiting for them to come to the house.

"They really could have waited," Duncan said.

"I know dear," Lisa said, kissing him deeply, making the big man turn red in the face, and Patty cleared her throat a couple of times.

"What was that for?" Duncan sputtered.

"Just because," Lisa said smiling.

"Some kind of just because," Sgt. Smith grumped, embarrassed at the public display of affection.

"You better watch it Sgt. Smith, I'll have Patty tackle you again," Duncan said, enjoying how Sgt. Smith turned red in the face as Patty sputtered.

"It's good to be home!" Sandra said, getting close to the porch steps.

The entire Homestead had encircled the people from the chopper, now split to the sides so they could all come up. Blake, Sandra and a man and woman nobody knew approached. They hugged their parents deeply, whispering to them. After a moment, Blake and Sandra sat, Chris in Sandra's arms now, getting the wind squeezed out of her. The man and woman sat as well.

"Well shucks," Blake said, squirming as almost four hundred eyes bored holes into them.

The whispers and talking was excited and it was hard to hear. Somebody hissed "sssssssshhhhhhhh-hhhhhhhhhh" and soon the crowd settled down, many people sat down in the grass.

In the distance, the helicopter pilots sat as well, men and a woman on the edges of the open bays of the Huey.

"This is Governor Hines to my left," Blake said, indicating the man, "And his assistant Miss Patricia Wisemer, formerly Governor Davis's aide, who was instrumental in bringing vital info to the panel."

Just weeks ago, having the Governor present would have elicited hostile glares, but the air had a

THE WORLD COWERS

festival quality to it and everyone cheered.

"Now, here's what I couldn't say over the air…"

Blake and Sandra took turns with the Governor, filling them in what it took for them to get a Presidential pardon. Blake had agreed on taking on the role of FEMA director, hopefully turning the public's impression of the camps around. They admitted there were camps where abuse ran rampant, but not the two camps in Kentucky to date.

They would open the camps up and let people stay or go as they pleased. They had worked out a rough plan on work for food. The component shortages were going to be a real issue as many of them were Chinese built, and with a state of War open with North Korea, China was rattling its sabers. Nobody wanted an all-out shooting war with China, but things were starting to look like that was the direction it was headed. Instead, the components were coming in from manufacturers in some of the more stable regions of Mexico and Canada by electronics manufacturers who formerly had made circuit boards for the automotive industry. They were retooling, and soon people would have more than copper wire to wrap around generators.

The cities of Kentucky would be opened up for all who wanted to flee the violence. They would be settled in the suburbs surrounding the camps, or work centers, as they were going to call them. It was something new, something the President reluctantly agreed on, and Kentucky would be the first state to have this on a trial basis.

The new communities would have several members visiting the Homestead to learn and, in turn, go back and teach their communities. It wouldn't be enough, so Blake asked everybody for volunteers to go to the communities and work with them. Almost every able-bodied man, woman and child raised their hands, much to Blake's amusement.

"Can't let you all go!" Blake grumbled, "Besides, Sandra and Duncan here are going to be having a big job to do soon."

"My, uh…" Duncan said, tapping his chest.

"You're on the organizational end. I want you to be our go-between with the higher up military officials. Dumb it down so a country hillbilly can understand them, and vice versa. Besides, they have a cardiologist who's waiting to see you soon," Blake told him and turned, and didn't have a lot of time before he was overwhelmed with questions.

"Sandra's going to be working with members of Sgt. Smith's team. Between her and three others she told me about, we're going to be training a civilian militia, similar to Sandra's squad—"

"Oh yeah!" a kid yelled and everybody cheered, making him sit down red faced.

"The threat from the Southwest is real. Most of us won't be involved in the fight directly, but here in the heartland we can train, supply, teach others and support the nation as it pulls itself back together. I'm supposed to continue Rebel Radio, and David here," Blake said pointing behind him, "Is about to get some new communications toys to play with. Sorry Patty, I may need to steal you to go with me and Sgt. Smith when we travel."

"That's no problem with me," Sgt. Smith said, looking at Patty who turned crimson and then kicked him in the shin, making him hop around on one leg.

Everybody busted up laughing at that.

"This place is about to get busy and we're going to be swamped with people soon, ready for training. Bobby, Melissa."

"Yes?" Bobby yelled from the side, drawing Blake's attention.

"You two have done wonders with the census and keeping things organized. I'd like for you to keep doing that. You're both in charge of getting background information, making teams," they both nodded...

"Mom?" Blake asked, turning to Lisa.

"Yes?"

"I need you to teach people basic food storage. I know that doesn't sound like a lot, but it's what you've been doing already, now with just an audience. We're going to set up some space outside here for you to work with others."

"You can count on me, son," she beamed.

"Wow, what's happened to him?" Duncan asked Lisa quietly. "He doesn't sound like the same man who left here."

"I think he finally gave up his insecurities," Lisa whispered back, taking Duncan's hand and squeezing it.

"Sgt. Smith, Corinne?" Blake yelled.

Both answered from different points of the crowd.

"You are going to be with me when we travel. One unit of each, military and civilian. I sort of think we might as well combine them anyways, since many of your groups are already uh…. a thing?" Blake said but they both smiled and nodded.

"Things are going to get really interesting really fast," Sandra shouted, startling everyone.

Her size made people underestimate her at first, but the voice that came forth bellowed and carried without the need of a megaphone. A trait she shared with her father.

"We've got less than a month to train up our trainers and find a place for us to start working with the volunteer militia. It'll be just like the Homestead in principal. You work, you eat. You fight, you win. Does that sound fair?"

The crowd shouted a resounding yes and everyone was crying, clapping and laughing.

"Now," Blake said, his voice carrying over the crowd, "The guy who had a working iPod in the bunker has loaned it to me along with some speakers to go with it. If that won't work, we'll pull an APC up here," Blake shouted, "And have us one good party."

"I thought he said he wasn't a leader," Hines whispered to Pamela Wisemer, who'd been briefed on everything before and after.

"The good ones are those who don't want it," she whispered back, her words almost lost in the noise and excitement of the crowd.

"Unlike Davis," Hines whispered.

"Maybe like you too," she said, poking him in the chest and she stood, holding her hand out to him.

"What's this?" Sandra asked, pulling her man to her feet also.

"You said something about a party," Pamela said loudly, "I want a dance!"

The men all started shouting offers to dance, as the men in the Huey keyed up the music.

"No, the first dance is mine," Hines told them all, but even he was smiling.

With so much uncertainty and a very real war squeezing the country from both sides, it was hard to have moments of fun, but even the phoenix rises out of the ashes, so shall America one day.

—THE END—

ABOUT THE AUTHOR

Boyd Craven III was born and raised in Michigan, an avid outdoors-man who's always loved to read and write from a young age. When he isn't working outside on the farm, or chasing a household of kids, he's sitting in his Lazy Boy, typing away.

http://www.boydcraven.com/
Facebook: https://www.facebook.com/boydcraven3
Email: boyd3@live.com
You can find the rest of Boyd's books on Amazon:
http://www.amazon.com/-/e/B00BANIQLG

39946554R00064